BOLD KIDS

CHILDREN'S AMERICAN LOCAL HISTORY BOOK

No part of this book may be reproduced or used in any way or form or by any means whether electronic or mechanical, this means that you cannot record or photocopy any material ideas or tips that are provided in this book.
Copyright 2022

All images in this book have been reproduced with the knowledge and prior consent of the artists concerned, and no responsibility is accepted by producer, publisher, or printer for any infringement of copyright or otherwise, arising from the contents of this publication.

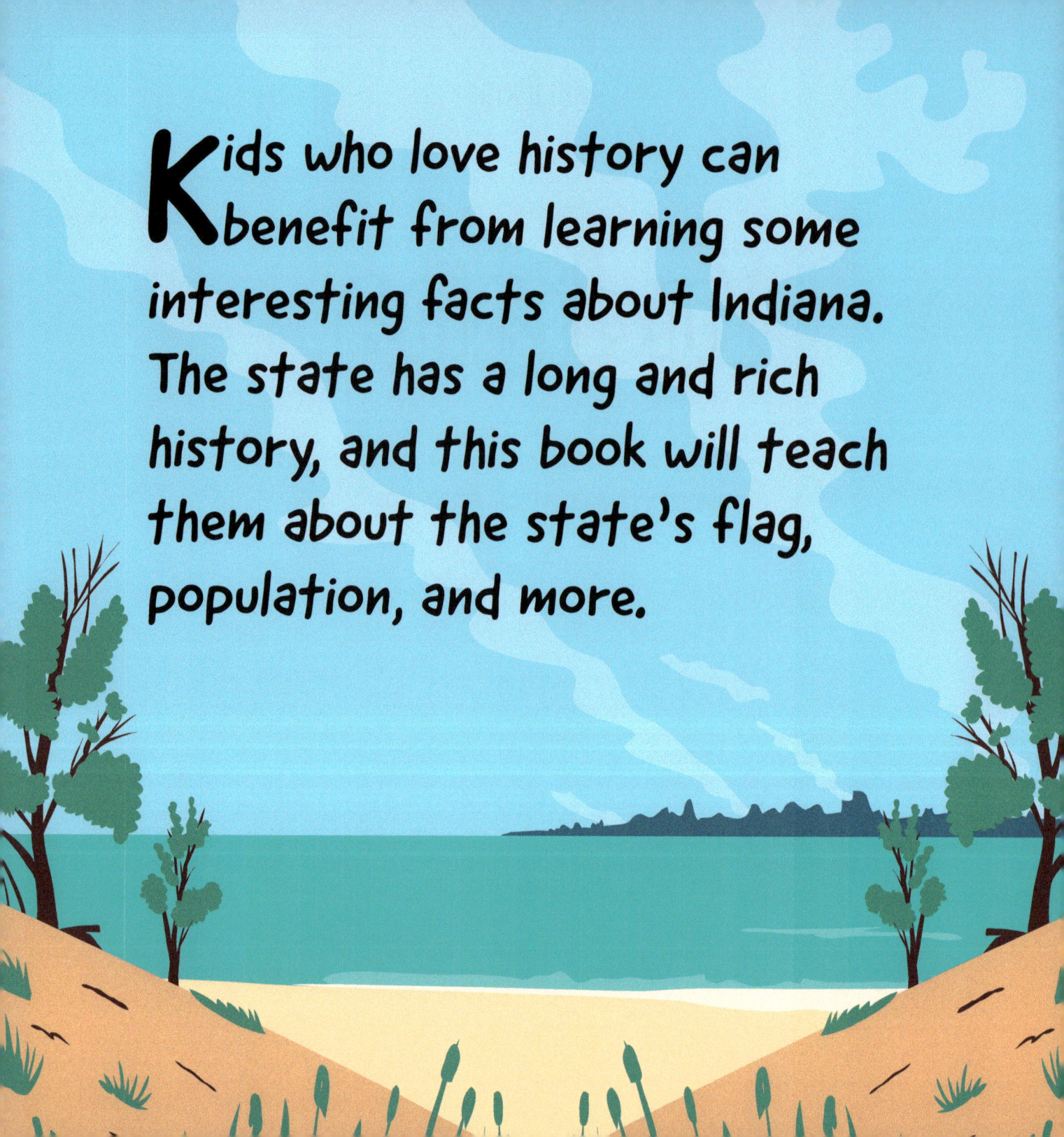

Kids who love history can benefit from learning some interesting facts about Indiana. The state has a long and rich history, and this book will teach them about the state's flag, population, and more.

In 1614, Frenchmen landed in Indiana. After the French took control of the area, the English invaded and occupied the region. The famous explorers Lewis and Clark left from their base in Clarksville, Indiana.

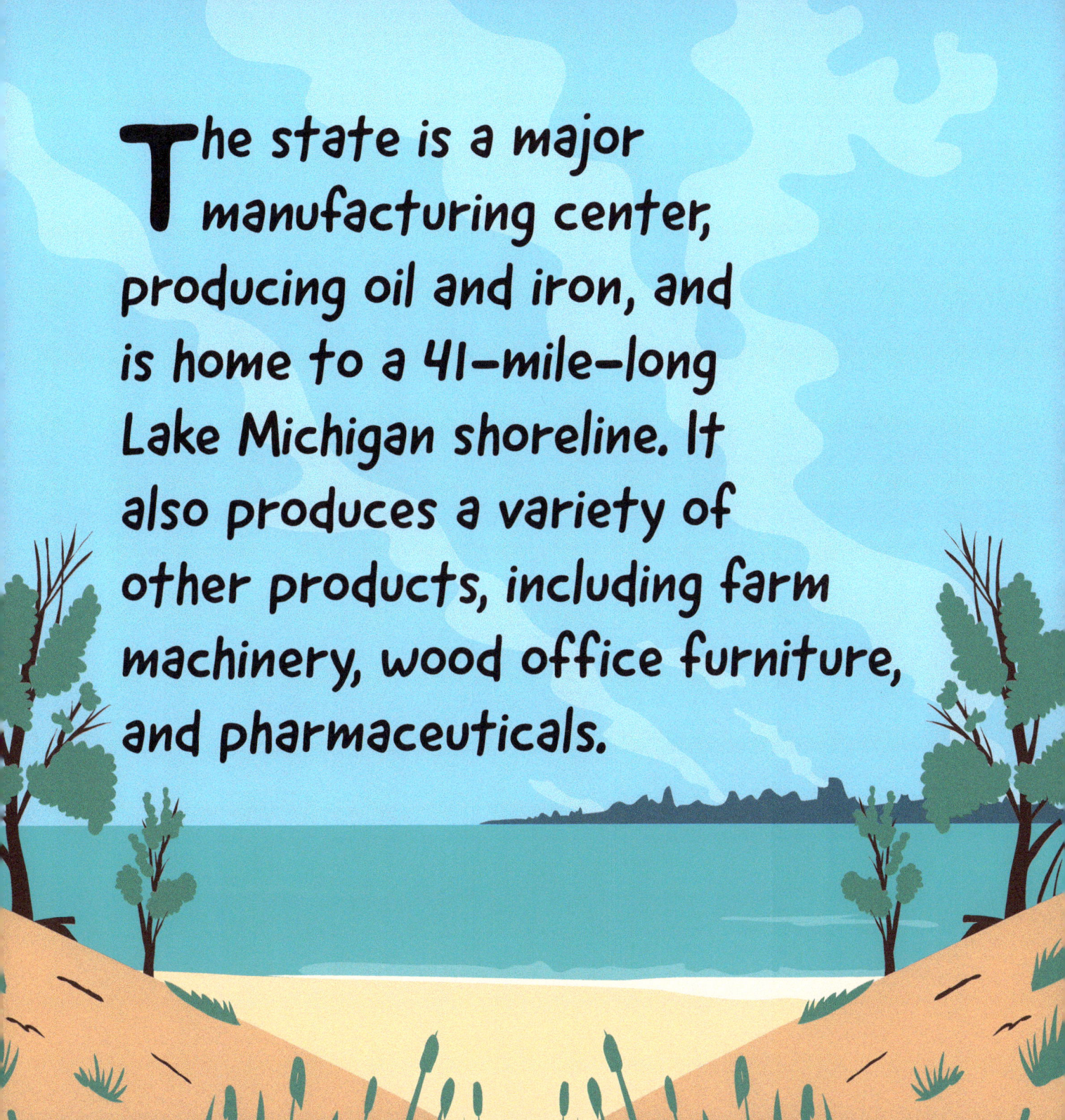

The state is a major manufacturing center, producing oil and iron, and is home to a 41-mile-long Lake Michigan shoreline. It also produces a variety of other products, including farm machinery, wood office furniture, and pharmaceuticals.

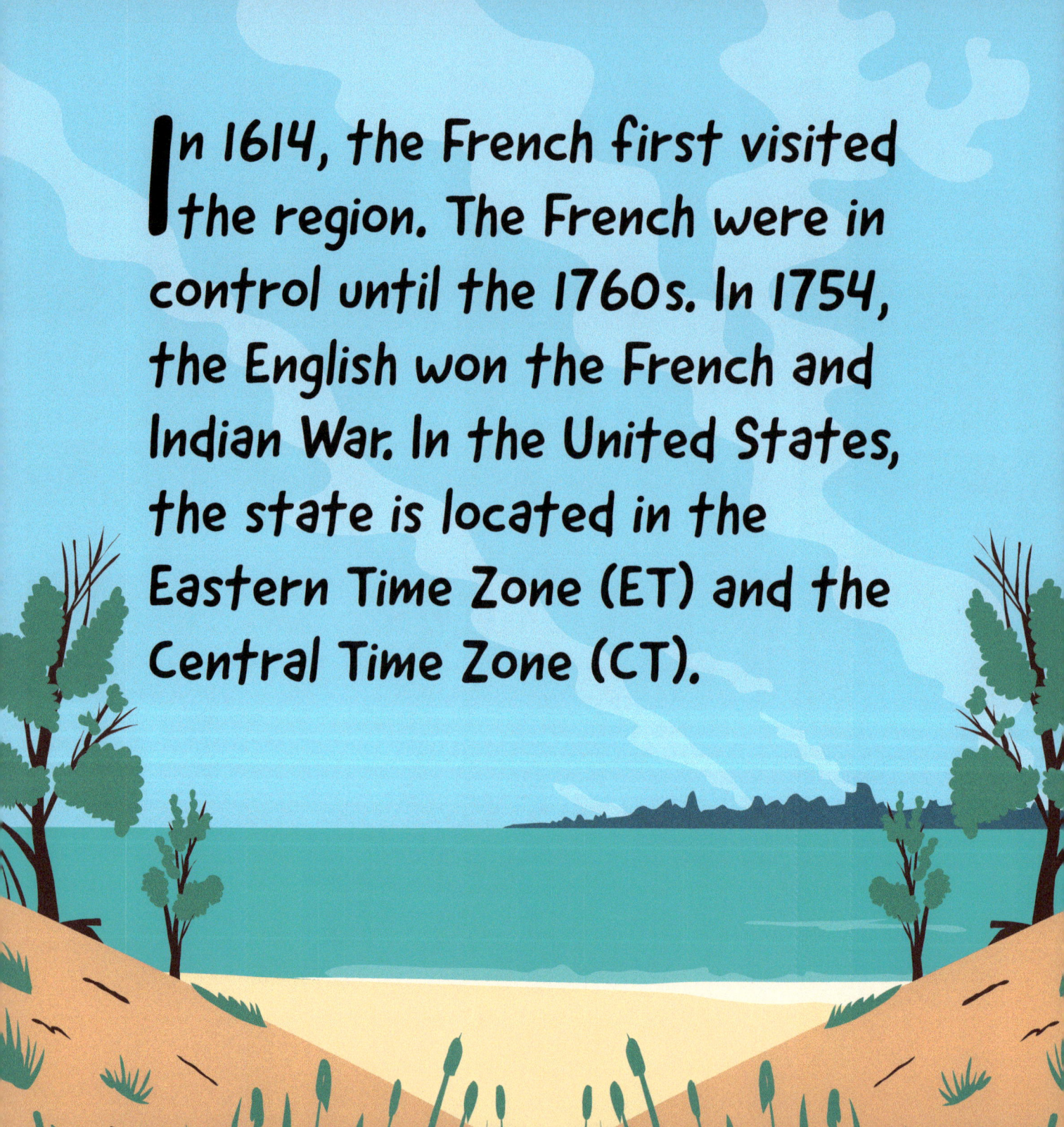

In 1614, the French first visited the region. The French were in control until the 1760s. In 1754, the English won the French and Indian War. In the United States, the state is located in the Eastern Time Zone (ET) and the Central Time Zone (CT).

The state's postal abbreviation is IN. The state's official flower and tree are the peony, tulip, and firefly. The cardinal is the state bird.

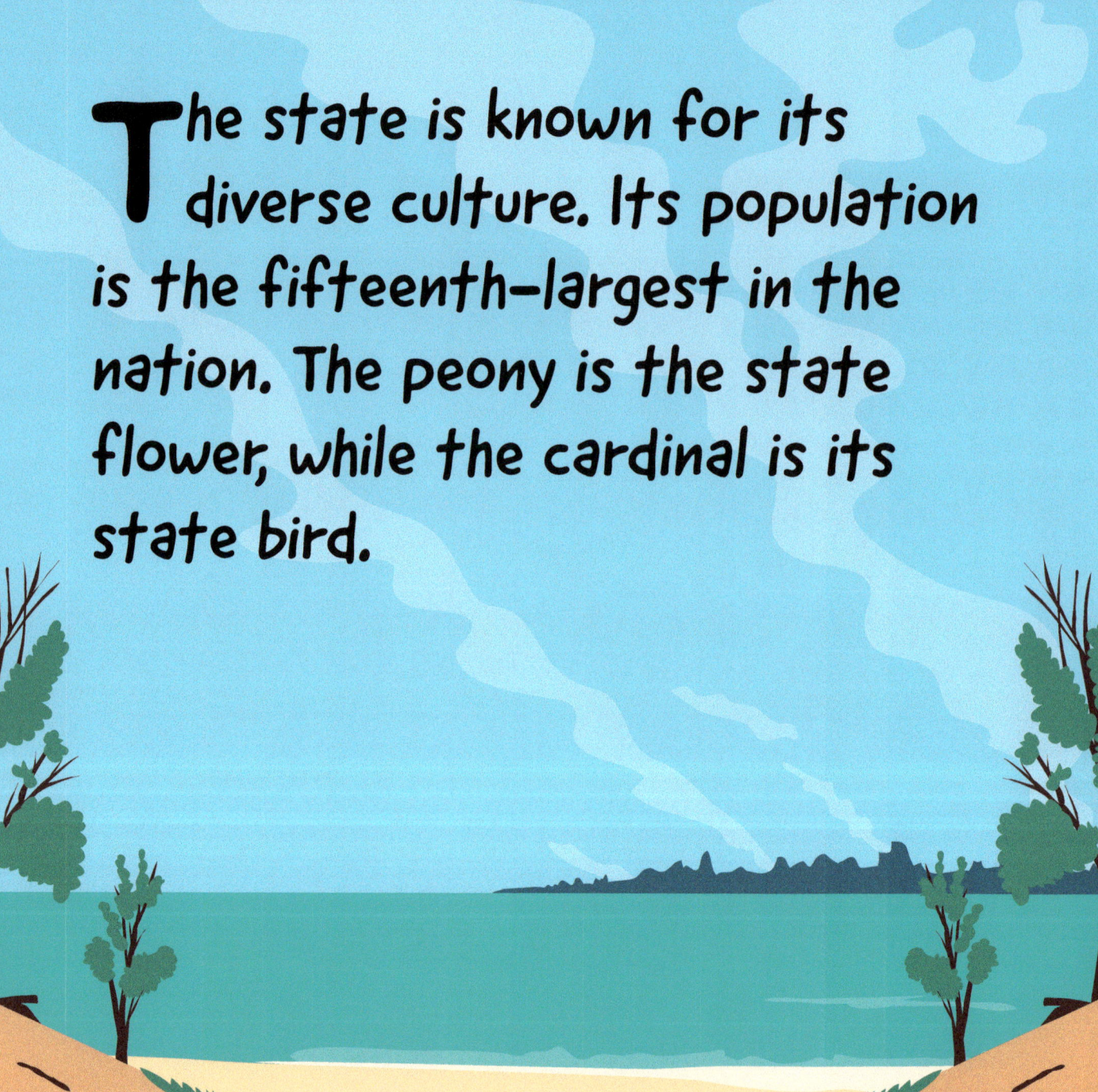

The state is known for its diverse culture. Its population is the fifteenth-largest in the nation. The peony is the state flower, while the cardinal is its state bird.

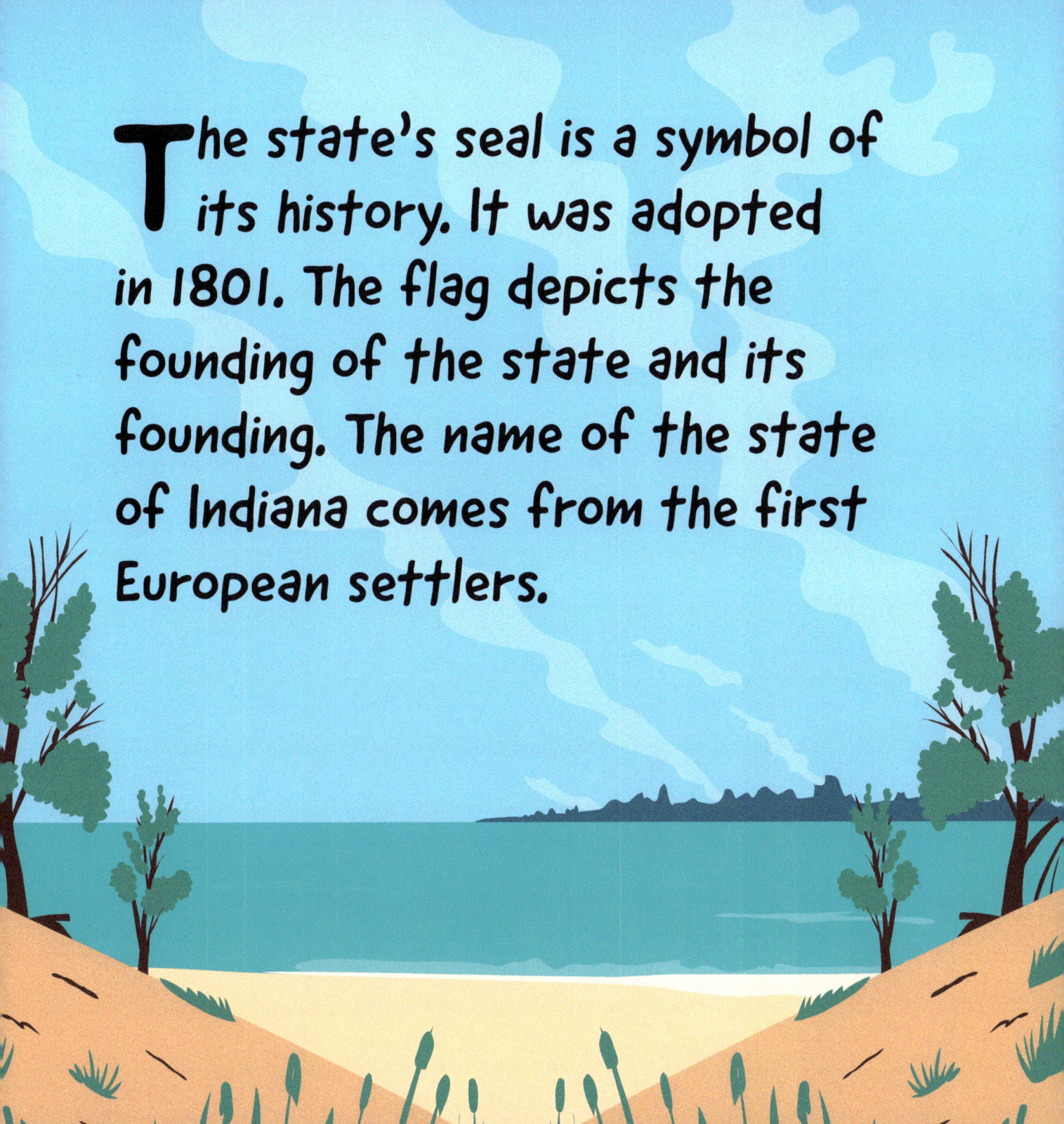

The state's seal is a symbol of its history. It was adopted in 1801. The flag depicts the founding of the state and its founding. The name of the state of Indiana comes from the first European settlers.

Indiana is the 15th-largest state in the country. The state is home to the Indianapolis Motor Speedway and several professional sports teams.

When the United States was formed, Indiana was the nineteenth state to join. In the same year, the state had two constitutions. The first one was adopted in 1816. In the second, it was adopted in 1821.

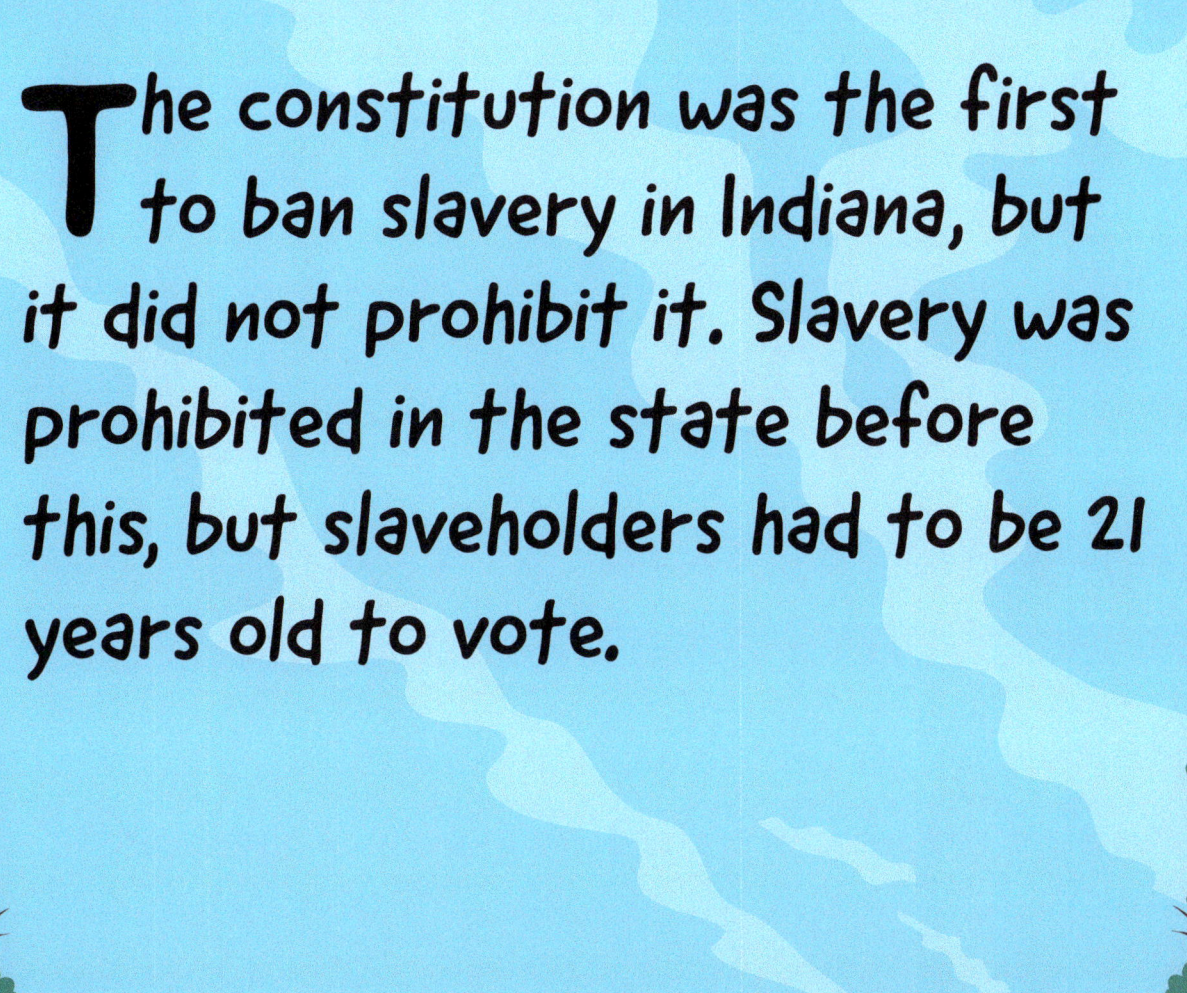

The constitution was the first to ban slavery in Indiana, but it did not prohibit it. Slavery was prohibited in the state before this, but slaveholders had to be 21 years old to vote.

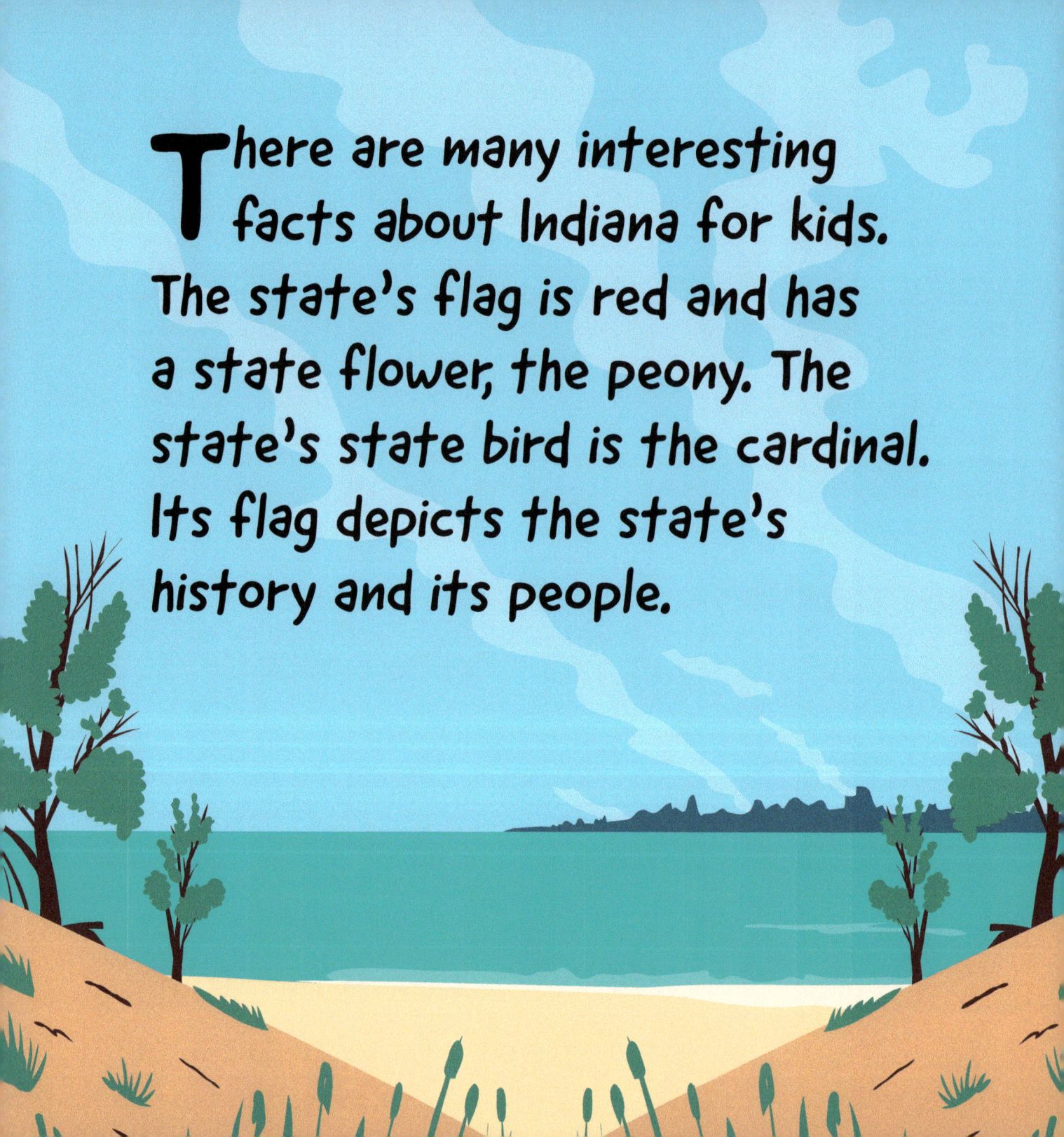

There are many interesting facts about Indiana for kids. The state's flag is red and has a state flower, the peony. The state's state bird is the cardinal. Its flag depicts the state's history and its people.

The flags are beautiful, and the sycamores are among the most beautiful in the world. The moonlit rivers and forests are a great way to learn more about the history of this beautiful state.

In terms of population, Indiana ranks 15th in the nation. With a population of 6,483,802, Indiana is the largest state in the midwest. The state's state bird and flower are the cardinal and peony, respectively.

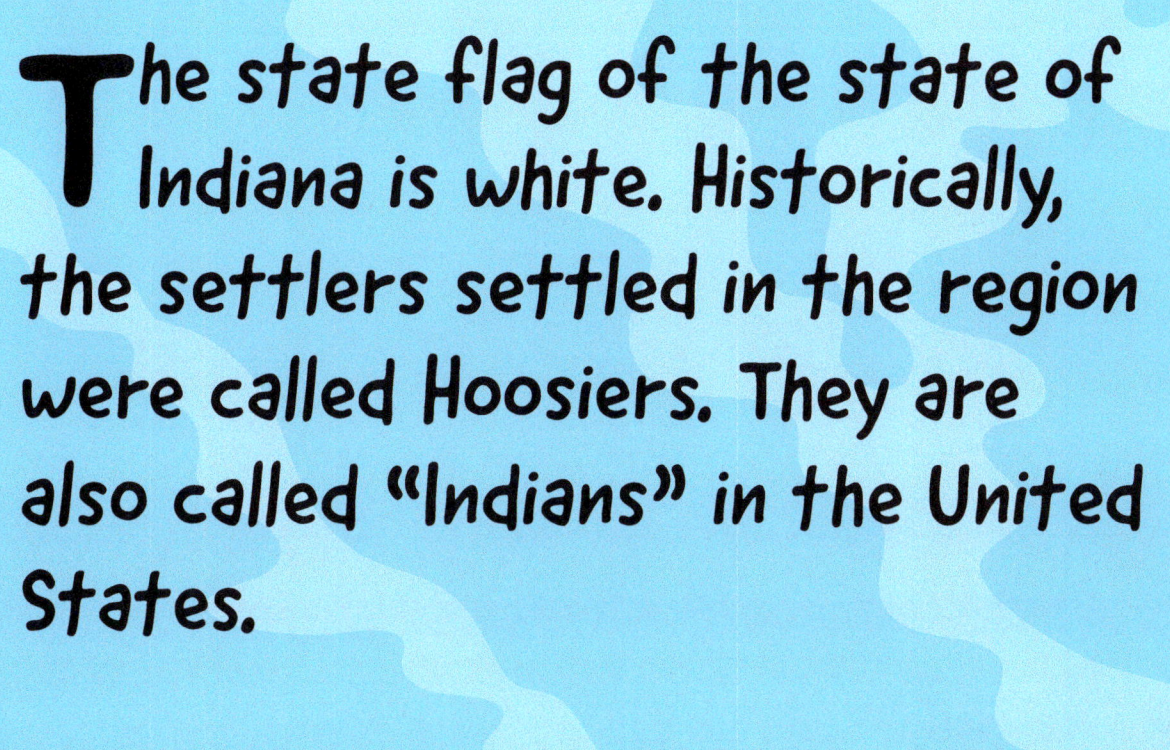

The state flag of the state of Indiana is white. Historically, the settlers settled in the region were called Hoosiers. They are also called "Indians" in the United States.

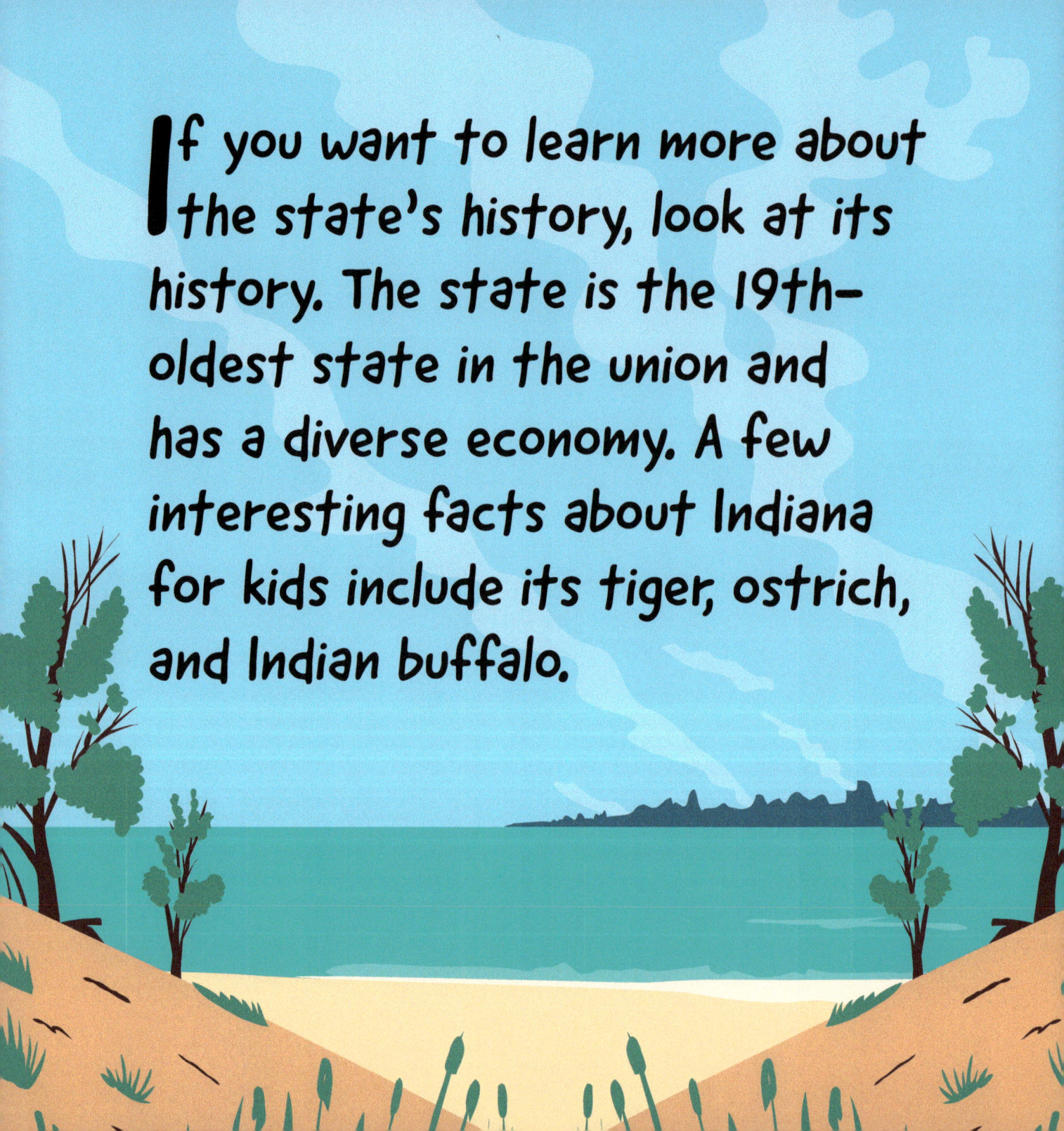

If you want to learn more about the state's history, look at its history. The state is the 19th-oldest state in the union and has a diverse economy. A few interesting facts about Indiana for kids include its tiger, ostrich, and Indian buffalo.

The flags of the other states are colorful and depict the country's history. This article will teach your children some interesting facts about Indiana.

There are nearly 100 historic covered bridges in Indiana. Ten thousand covered bridges were built in the United States during the 1800s, but only eighty-five are still standing.

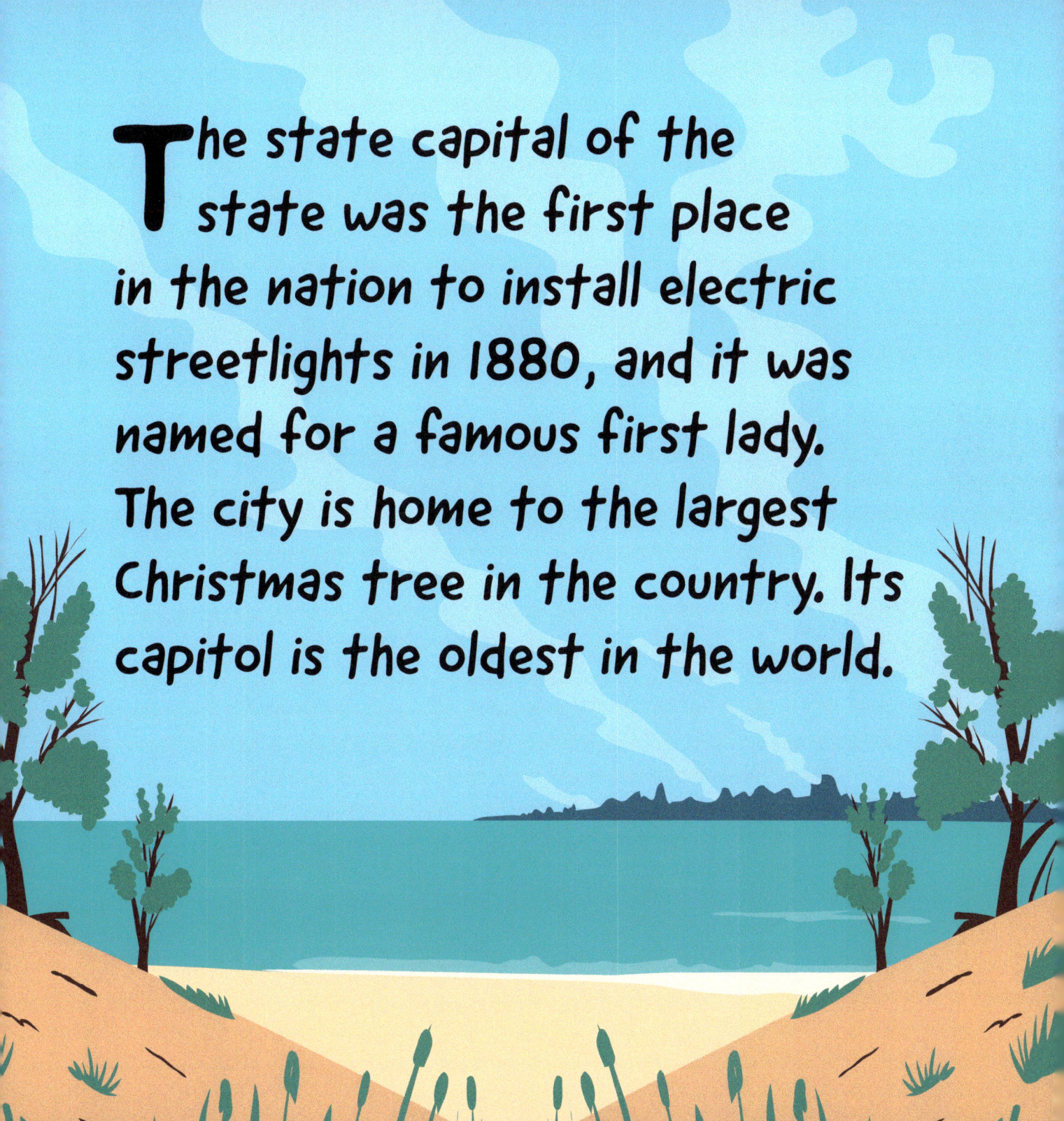

The state capital of the state was the first place in the nation to install electric streetlights in 1880, and it was named for a famous first lady. The city is home to the largest Christmas tree in the country. Its capitol is the oldest in the world.

Lightning Source UK Ltd.
Milton Keynes UK
UKHW050837210223
417371UK00008B/117